W9-BCT-071

Bouki Dances the Kokioko

A COMICAL TALE FROM HAITI

Diane Wolkstein

ILLUSTRATED BY Jesse Sweetwater

GULLIVER BOOKS
HARCOURT BRACE & COMPANY
SAN DIEGO   NEW YORK   LONDON

For Regina Ress, wondrous dancer, sterling friend
—D. W.

For my mother, Donna O'Hare,
who first sat me down with paint and paper
—J. S.

Text copyright © 1997, 1978 by Diane Wolkstein
Illustrations copyright © 1997 by Jesse Sweetwater

Library of Congress Cataloging-in-Publication Data
Wolkstein, Diane.
Bouki dances the Kokioko: a comical tale from Haiti/
retold by Diane Wolkstein; illustrated by Jesse Sweetwater.
"Gulliver Books."
p. cm.
Summary: After much coaching, Bouki wins the prize for dancing
the king's secret dance but is then outwitted by his sneaky friend.
ISBN 0-15-200034-8
[1. Folklore—Haiti.] I. Sweetwater, Jesse, ill. II. Title.
PZ8.1.W84Bo 1997
398.2'097294—dc20
[E] 95-39314

Printed in Singapore

First edition
A C E F D B

The illustrations in this book were done with liquid acrylics,
watercolor, and gouache on Arches watercolor paper.
The display type was set in Fontesque.
The text type was set in Neue Neuland Light.
Color separations by Chromavision Colour Separation (Pte) Ltd., Singapore
Printed and bound by Tien Wah Press, Singapore
This book was printed on totally chlorine-free Nymolla Matte Art paper.
Production supervision by Stanley Redfern
Designed by Lydia D'moch

About the Story

When I traveled to Haiti in 1972, I was delighted to discover an active, rich storytelling tradition. When the moon was full or on Saturday nights, farmers would gather outside their thatched-roof huts and exchange stories. Storytellers, men and women of all ages, would call out *"Cric?"* to the gathered group. The storyteller who received the assenting *"Crac!,"* indicating that the group was eager to hear his or her story, would begin. Everyone in the audience would join in on the songs. For five years I returned to Haiti to take part in this experience. Slowly I learned Creole and was able to follow the stories. But when a story was too complex for me to follow, secure that my tape recorder was at work, I would bask in the sounds of the Haitian night and the pleasure of people gathered together enjoying stories.

One of the most exciting storytelling nights I attended took place in 1974 in Carrefort-Dufort, a small sugarcane district west of Port-au-Prince. The storytellers were "hot"; the crowd was extremely responsive. Everyone was eager to tell a story. Edouard, a young farmer in his early twenties with an infectious laugh, a few missing teeth, and a great enjoyment of life, was the fourth to perform that evening. He told "Bouki Dances the Kokioko." When he danced the first part of the Kokioko, he held himself erect, his right hand under his right breast, and swayed his upper chest from side to side—a bit like a rooster. When he came to the *"Samba dance"* section of the song, he clapped and turned around and around, his eyes twinkling. Sometimes Edouard's words would get lost because he would start laughing almost every time he mentioned the prankster Malice, but by the time he came to the last song—*"If you have no sense/Put your sack on the ground/And dance"*—we were all singing and laughing with him.

"Cric?"

— D. W.

There was once a king of Haiti who loved dancing. He loved dancing more than anything else in the world. If he could, he would have invited dancers to perform for him every evening of the week. Unfortunately, he did not have enough money in his treasury to pay for them.

One evening after dinner the king was sitting in the garden and a song came to him:

Kokioko, oh Samba.
Ah, la, la. Ah, la, la, la, la.
Kokioko, oh Samba.
Ah, la, la. Ah, la, la, la, la.

The king sang his song several times. Then, sniffing the soft night air, he stood up. Swaying back and forth, the king slowly began to make up a dance to accompany his song:

Kokioko, oh Samba.
Now I dance, now I dance like this.
Samba oh, Samba ah. Samba dance.

The king moved his chest from side to side. Next he added his arms and hips. When it came to *Samba dance,* he clapped his hands and turned in a circle. The king was very pleased with his dance.

No dancer could make up such a wonderful dance, he thought. *But, of course, there are always those who think they can do anything.* Just then the king understood how he could continue to watch dancing every night while keeping his treasury full.

The next morning the king announced that he would pay five thousand gourdes to anyone who could dance the Kokioko. No one had any idea what the Kokioko was. But that evening a long line of dancers waited outside the palace, hoping they might

be able to guess the steps of the king's dance. That night the
king saw some of the most splendid dancing he had ever seen,
and all for free—for no one was able to guess the steps of the
Kokioko.

The next night it was the same thing, and the night after that. Once a young woman happened to do the first steps of the Kokioko, swaying her chest to the left and then to the right. The king sat up in excitement. But then the woman clapped in the second section instead of during *Samba dance*. Another time a young man moved his chest, arms, and hips as the king had done, but he didn't clap his hands for the last part.

Months passed. The king watched dancer after dancer and never tired of the music or the dancing. But always, after the dancers and servants left for the evening, the king danced the Kokioko by himself so he would not forget it.

Well, one evening after working all day, Malice, the king's gardener, was on his way home when he realized that he had forgotten his straw hat. He needed it to protect himself from the bright morning sun, so he returned to the palace. As Malice approached the garden, he heard someone singing the Kokioko

song. He wondered who could be singing, for the hopeful dancers had already gone home. As Malice came closer, he recognized the king's voice. Malice tiptoed even closer. The king was singing and dancing. Quickly Malice hid behind a tree and watched the king dance the Kokioko in the moonlight.

Malice followed the king's every movement with greedy, eager eyes. He did not move. He hardly breathed until the king had finished his dance and gone into the palace. Malice then ran home to show the steps of the Kokioko to his wife. Madame Malice was delighted with her clever husband, who explained how he intended to win the five thousand gourdes without even entering the contest.

The next morning Madame Malice woke her husband early, and they ate breakfast as the roosters were crowing. Before going to the palace, Malice went to visit his old friend Bouki.

"*Bou-ki,*" Malice said in a high, sweet voice, "you and I have been friends for years. You've always helped me. Now I want to do something *really* great for you."

"Oh-oh," said Bouki in his low, gruff voice. He had been friends with Malice long enough to know that you were better off before

Malice came along. No one was trickier than Malice.

"Oh, thank you, Malice," Bouki slowly answered. "But I—I really don't need any help."

"Bouki! Bouki!" Malice could not be stopped. "Do you know what I saw last night? I saw the king dancing the Kokioko in his garden."

"I saw every step he made," Malice continued. "I can't dance it, for I'm the king's servant and he would suspect me. But I can teach you the steps and *you* can win the five thousand gourdes."

Now, five thousand gourdes was a lot of money—especially for Bouki, who had many little Boukis to feed. It was also a lot of money for Malice, who had many little Malices.

"Show me the dance," said Bouki, forgetting the years of tricks Malice had played on him.

Malice danced and sang, *"Kokioko, oh Samba. Now I dance, now I dance like this—"*

Bouki tried to follow Malice's movements, but he was so fat and awkward, he nearly fell over.

Kokio-oh-oh-OH-H!

"Never mind," said Malice cheerfully. "I'll be back tonight to teach you. We'll do a little bit every night, and you'll learn."

Two months later Bouki and Malice joined the line of dancers waiting outside the king's palace. When it was Bouki's turn, he went in alone and danced for the king. It was a very fat dancer who danced the Kokioko, but it *was* the Kokioko!

There was no doubt about it. Bouki had moved his chest, his arms, his hips, had clapped and turned exactly as the king had done. The king was flabbergasted, amazed, stunned, and had no choice but to give Bouki his reward. Bouki rushed joyously out of the palace with his sack of five thousand gourdes.

"Malice, I've won, I've won!" Bouki shouted.
Malice and Bouki walked gaily home through the forest, but as
they passed a large breadfruit tree, Malice suddenly stopped and

said, "*Bou-ki,* now that you can do the Kokioko, I'm going to teach you one of the easiest dances there is."

"Great!" said Bouki.

Malice moved his rump, shook
his head, and sang:

If you have no sense,
Put your sack on the ground
And dance.

"Oh, that's easy," said Bouki, "especially for someone who knows how to dance." Bouki put his sack on the ground. He moved his rump, shook his head, and sang.

"Good," said Malice. "Now, faster!"

Malice closed his eyes, threw his arms in the air, and danced and sang faster and faster:

> If you have no sense,
> Put your sack on the ground
> And dance.

"Oh, I can do that," Bouki said, and he, too, closed his eyes, threw his arms in the air, shook his whole body, and danced with Malice. Bouki's eyes were shut tight when Madame Malice crept

out from behind the breadfruit tree. Quietly she picked up Bouki's sack and tiptoed back into the woods as Malice and Bouki continued to sing, *"If you have no sense—"*

A branch in the woods cracked. Bouki opened his eyes and looked at the ground. His sack was gone.

"*My sack!* Malice, my SACK!"

"*Bouki,* did you put it on the ground?" Malice asked.

"Yes, of course I did," said Bouki.

"Oh, Bou-ki, no. I *tried* to warn you," said Malice. And he
disappeared into the night, singing:

> *If you have no sense,*
> *Put your sack on the ground*
> *And dance.*

Unfamiliar Words in the Story

Bouki (BOO-kee) A well-known character in Haitian folklore. It is considered an insult in Creole to call another person a Bouki, meaning a "dummy."

"Cric?"—"Crac!" (kreek-krak) A call-and-response dialogue between a storyteller and his or her audience that precedes the telling of a story. *Cric?* means "Are you ready?" *Crac!* means "Go!"

gourde (GORD) The standard denomination of Haitian currency. The similarity between the Haitian gourde and the word *gourd,* meaning a squashlike fruit, is not coincidental. Before paper money was used in Haiti, the calabash—a kind of tropical fruit, or gourd—was exchanged for goods. Sixteen gourdes are worth approximately one dollar.

Kokioko (KOH-kee-oh-koh) An onomatopoeic word that imitates the crowing sound made by a rooster, similar to the American *cock-a-doodle-doo.*

Malice (Mah-LEES) A trickster character who frequently appears in Haitian folklore. Because of his insatiable desire to have more for himself, Malice always tries to outwit others. The name derives from the French word *malice,* meaning "evil intention."

samba (SAM-bah) A dance of African origin that has a step-close-step-close pattern. The samba dancer dips and springs upward on each beat of the music. Also a word of African origin meaning lead singer. The samba was often the person who led the singing when groups of farmers worked together bringing in the harvest.